Now You're Talking

SMART TALK

Now You're Talking

Winning with Words

Ami Havens

Troll Associates

Library of Congress Cataloging-in-Publication Data

Havens, Ami.
　　Now you're talking / by Ami Havens; illustrated by Donald Richey.
　　　　p.　　cm.—(Smart talk)
　　Summary: Discusses the importance of communicating through talking
and gives tips on how to talk and listen more effectively.
　　ISBN 0-8167-2142-4 (lib. bdg.)　　　ISBN 0-8167-2143-2 (pbk.)
　　1. Parent and child—United States—Juvenile literature.
2. Communication in the family—United States—Juvenile literature.
[1. Communication.　2. Parent and child]　I. Richey, Donald, ill.
II. Title.　III. Series.
HQ755.85.H39　1991
306.874—dc20　　　　　　　　　　　　　　　　90-10764

Table of Contents

Let's Talk

I sn't it great to have someone to talk to? Someone who truly understands you? You know,
someone who loves you and really listens to you—
someone you can open up to without a lot of
misunderstandings.

That's how most of us want to feel about talking to
our parents. And maybe most of the time you talk

with your parents you do feel that way. But maybe there are times when it seems like your parents are on another planet—or you just wish they were, because they *just don't understand*. And when that happens, it's a good bet that poor communicating is at least part of the problem.

Why does it seem like they always say "no" before you've even asked the question? Why do they still treat you like you're a little kid? Can't they give you a little freedom? Why are they so unreasonable— and why do they seem so unfair sometimes?

Well, there are probably a lot of reasons for what happens in your family—and sometimes all of us get busy or distracted and don't treat each other the way we really want to. But you can help by learning to talk to your parents in ways that help them under- stand you better—and that's what this book is all about! We're going to be talking about talking!

(We're going to use the word "parents" and talk a lot about "moms" and "dads" but we understand that lots of families don't fit that pattern. Just sub- stitute the person or people that fit your situation.)

There will be lots of chances for you to have fun as we go along, with plenty of true-to-life examples in each chapter, and some quizzes to let you know how you're doing. You won't be able to write in this book, so why not get a special notebook, just for yourself—your own journal! In fact, throughout this book, we'll show you how a journal can help you tackle a number of situations.

Talk Talk

Why is talking so important? You've probably noticed that bad things don't seem so bad when you share them, and good things seem even more special when you can tell a good friend or a family member about them. Somehow, when you sit down with a friend and tell her how mean another friend has been to you, the incident itself doesn't matter anymore; what matters is that you have a real friend who will listen. Or when that cute guy you've been passing notes to all term finally sends one back, it's great to be able to run home and tell your sister, who will be just as excited as you are.

Why does talking help so much? People need people—it's that simple. No one is happy living alone, without the love and concern of others. And talking is how we get in touch with the people around us. It's how we share feelings and really learn to understand each other.

If you don't believe talking is important—just think of the impact of hearing those three little words, "I love you!"

TALK IT OVER—AND IT'S BETTER

Jennifer's "gray day" is a good example of how talking helps. Jennifer thought it was just about the worst day of her life, really awful, YUCK in capital letters. She had found out her best friend was giving a party and hadn't invited her, and was so upset about it that she wasn't listening in class. When her favorite teacher called on her, she didn't know the *question*, much less the answer. And then she realized she'd left her new sweater in the lunchroom, and when she went back to look for it she discovered it was gone.

By the time she got home, Jennifer was in tears, feeling like the lowest of the low. Both her parents were at work, and there was no one at home to make her feel better. But Jennifer couldn't take being alone with her misery, so she called her mother and told her what a bad day she'd had. Her mother sympathized, and by the end of the conversation Jennifer felt a whole lot better. She'd still had a bad day—but she wasn't alone. Someone had listened to her and had understood how she felt. And that simple fact really helped! Talking it over with an adult who loved her helped Jennifer cope with her gray day.

TALK KEEPS TRACK

Talking does other things, too, some of them complicated, and others a lot simpler. Through talking, we let people know what we need, what we think, what things we are willing to share and what things are off limits. Talking can also help us understand our feelings. It stirs up our thoughts, and helps put them in a presentable form. Have you ever heard that line, "How do I know how I feel until I hear what I say?" Well, it's true!

Chances are the people you talk to most about the important things are your family. Which brings us to the tricky part—sometimes these people who are so important to us can be the most difficult to talk to. Why? Because they're the people we know the best and that can make it hard. Sometimes we're afraid to tell them our fears or concerns, afraid that they'll think less of us. Or we're afraid that they won't understand—and if *they* don't understand, who will?

Talking can also be difficult if we have a problem that we're embarrassed about: Maybe it's a taboo subject or maybe we feel that we should already know the answer, and so we don't want to discuss it. We're afraid that if we do, our parents will see us as less strong and confident than we would like to be seen. Or we might be afraid that they will punish us for talking about something, or that they're simply too old-fashioned or too busy to understand.

So, for a lot of complicated reasons, sometimes it's most difficult to talk to the people we love the most—our parents. We'll talk more about this in the following chapters, but before we do, let's talk about the ways we can do more than talk: the ways we can communicate. Because, in spite of how difficult it is, communicating is really, really important.

LEARNING TO TALK

What's surprising is that as important as communicating is, no one teaches us to do it. Once you've grasped the rudiments of language and have learned your ABC's, people seem to figure you'll get the trick of really communicating all by yourself. Maybe there ought to be a class at school, Beginning Communication, required for graduation. After all, talking is *hard*—saying not just any words, but saying the *right* words, really communicating your ideas and feelings.

Where are we supposed to learn this stuff? And when?

Well, we think everyone can learn to be a better communicator, and we think the place and time to start is here and now. So, let's look at what communicating—talking—is all about.

There are some basic rules about talking. These rules hold true no matter who is talking to whom or what they're talking about. We also think you should know about what we call the "Dreadful Exaggerators" and the "I Factor." If you can learn the basics, avoid the Dreadful Exaggerators and control the I Factor, you'll be a top talker in a flash!

THE BASICS

The first basic is that *talking is a two-way street*. It's not something you do to someone or that someone does to you, and you can't do it by yourself. (You can talk to yourself, but that's not real communication.) Communicating requires at least two people, a talker and a listener—and both are *equally* important.

The second thing to remember is that *talking is not a contest or a game*—no one "wins" a conversation, even if that conversation sounds like an argument. The goal of communicating is understanding, not getting your own way.

Talkers and listeners must be able to change places if they really want to communicate—this is the third basic. Each has to respect the other's rights and dignity. That's because good communication means being able to put yourself in the other's position. Even if you don't agree with someone's viewpoint, you should try to imagine you're them and see it from their point of view. In talking, as in most things, if you treat others like you want to be treated, you'll find things go a lot better.

The fourth basic is simple: *Pick a good time and place to talk*. Times to avoid are when everyone is too busy to concentrate, like in the morning when you're rushing to get out the door to school. And if you are really angry, it's often best to wait until you can cool down enough to talk and listen quietly. Also, if you're not exactly sure what you want to talk about—wait until you figure it out a little! Just be sure you don't put off talking too long, or keep finding reasons not to do it—pick a good time, but make it soon.

The two key things to look for in a place to talk are privacy and the lack of distraction. You should be able to talk fully and comfortably, with everybody involved, and without worrying about anyone over-hearing you or making you feel self-conscious. Sometimes this means you should pick a room that has a door. Sometimes a public place where no one is paying any attention to you is better. If you want the whole family to be involved, choose a time and place when everyone will be around. If you want it to be just you and your mom, figure out when everyone else will be away. And you should never be doing anything else while talking. Wait until after dinner. Turn off the TV. Feed the dog later. Talking requires your full concentration.

Some Good Places to Talk

- *At the dinner table after a meal*

- *In your room*

- *In your parent's study*

- *In a park*

- *By the side of the pool*

- *In the laundry room*

THE DREADFUL EXAGGERATORS

The Dreadful Exaggerators are two loaded words you should avoid using. Once we tell you what they are, we think you'll realize their inherent dangers. OK, ready? **ALWAYS** and **NEVER.** We bet you can think of lots of times you've heard these words used in arguments—maybe you've even used them yourself. Well, don't: They just get in the way! Like when your mom says "You *never* listen," or you say to your dad "You *always* criticize me"—probably not true, huh? Don't accuse people, just stick with the facts.

THE I FACTOR

And now for the biggie: It's simple, but it's critical. If, whenever you talk from now on, you keep this one idea in mind, you'll be set. This is it: *Emphasize "I" and not "you" when you're talking about how you feel.*

Doesn't sound so big to you? Not worth all the build-up? Well, just think about it for a minute. What if your mom said, "I'd like to see your room cleaned up today—it really makes me feel upset to see it such a mess," instead of "Your room is a mess—you haven't cleaned it up in ages, you just don't care, do you?" Or if your brother said, "I'd really like to watch some music videos tonight," instead of "You're hogging the television, you jerk." Or if you said to your dad, "I'd like to have some time to talk with you," instead of "You don't care what's happening to me."

If you learn to describe how you feel, instead of

11

focusing your words on the other person's character or behavior, you'll find that people listen to you and understand you better. And you'll probably find that they start doing it, too! The I Factor is so important because it can completely change the way you talk to the people around you—for the better!

THE PAYOFF TAKES PRACTICE

Like any important skill, good communicating takes practice. Don't expect it to come naturally or all at once. Think of it like skating or playing the guitar or learning math—you'll get it if you hang in there and keep trying.

Sometimes talking is difficult. When things are tough, when bad times come and we're sad or upset or disappointed, it can take work and courage to really stick with it. It's especially difficult when you're trying to resolve something in your family— that's when you have to remember that communicating is not about winning, it's about growing together and sharing together. Good communicating means learning about each other.

But at those times when communication seems more trouble than it's worth, stick with it! Families matter: It's worth the time it takes to learn to talk with each other.

Good communication can bring even the happiest family closer together.

KEEP TALKING

Communication is an ongoing process, just like washing the dishes and doing homework—even if you do a great job today, you'll have to do it again tomorrow! But don't be put off by that: Communication is worth working at!

Remember that class you *didn't* have in school? Beginning Communication? Well, guess what—your parents didn't have it either, and it's very probable that no one ever taught them how to communicate. Some parents just aren't good communicators, and if yours are of this variety, your job will be harder. You can still do it—and you should!—but until some of your new skills rub off on them, it may be slow going. Keep trying, you'll get there!

☆☆ Test Your Talking Skills ☆☆

What kind of talker are you? Find out with this quiz!

1. *Your mom says you can't go shopping with your friends because you have to stay with your little brother. You:*

    a. Say "You never let me do anything I want; you always ruin my life."

b. Run out of the room and refuse to discuss it.

c. Keep begging until everyone is miserable and you get your way or get grounded.

d. Explain to your mother that the shopping trip is important, and that you'd be willing to watch your brother later or take him with you.

2. *You find your diary on your desk, not in the drawer where you always leave it, and it's open. Your mom put laundry away in your room that day. You:*

   a. Say she's always snooping in your stuff and that she never trusts you.

   b. Bang your door shut and refuse to talk to your mother all evening.

   c. Tell her she'd better not do it again, start a new diary and find a safer hiding place.

   d. Explain to your mother how important your privacy is to you, and how hurt you feel when it is violated.

3. *You are shopping with your dad and you see a lamp that would look just great in your room. He says the lamp you have is fine. You:*

   a. Say he's a stingy person who always says

no, and he never lets you have anything you want.

   b. Stalk out of the store and go wait in the car by yourself.

   c. Keep begging until he gives in, or say you didn't want it anyway.

   d. Explain to your dad that you are trying to make your room look neater, that you've been looking for a new lamp for a while and that you will help pay for the lamp with your own money.

4. *Your mom says she is taking your sister with her on a sales trip out of town. You would like to go, too, but she says she can only take your sister this time. You:*

   a. Tell her she's mean and never lets you do anything you want to do, and your sister always gets her way.

   b. Bang your door shut and refuse to discuss it.

   c. Keep begging until she grounds you, or tell her you don't want to go on the stupid trip with her anyway.

   d. Explain that you'd really like some time with her, too, and that you feel left out.

5. *Your team has just won the soccer game, but you didn't get to play much. When you get home, your dad*

says that the team seems to do okay without you, and that you probably aren't fast enough to play. You:

  a. Say he's always criticizing you and he never says anything good about you.

  b. Refuse to talk to him.

  c. Tell him he's ruining your life, and you want to quit playing, anyway.

  d. Say that you enjoy playing and that you really feel hurt by his comment.

☆☆☆

Scoring:

If you answered mostly a's: You've adopted the Dreadful Exaggerators. Give them up and your talks will improve.

If you answered mostly b's: You're not talking at all. Try taking the time to find the words to express yourself—no one can read your mind.

If you answered mostly c's: You're trying to talk, but it's not working out too well. You just need to work on the communication skills described in this chapter and you'll be in great shape!

If you answered mostly d's: Great job! Your communicating skills are right on track!

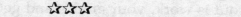

☆☆☆

Why Don't They Understand?

*D*oes it ever seem like your parents are just too old and out of it to understand how you feel? Are you puzzled by the music they like and the things they like to do? Does it seem that all they care about is work, your grades and getting you to keep your room clean? Or maybe they're really great most of the time, but sometimes they just won't leave you alone. Don't they understand?

We've got a surprise for you—your parents were kids once, too! And not that long from now, you are going to be an adult. So what? The point is that age *isn't* the point—what matters is that people need to talk to each other and understand each other, no matter how old they happen to be. And there are a lot of ways that you and your parents can get closer, no matter how far apart you seem now!

FIND A COMMON GROUND

Let's try a little experiment. Try getting your parents alone, and then convince them to tell you what they were like at your age. Ask them what they did for fun, what they used to do with their friends, what scared them or bothered them. Ask them what *they* thought of *their* parents. You might be surprised by what you hear! Once you have found a common ground—you both know what it's like to be growing up and dealing with your parents—you'll find that you have a good starting place for discussions.

You won't agree with your parents all the time—and they won't always agree with you—even after you talk things over! Sometimes, what you want

Find a common ground and learn just how much you share.

and what they want just won't be the same thing. But that's not the point, either. The point is to keep talking and growing together.

After all, we all get caught up in our daily lives and lose touch with the people around us. Sometimes we need to slow down, to listen to and observe what's happening *now*. Quick—what was your mother wearing yesterday? Did you notice? What's your dad's favorite music? What are your parents' favorite foods? If they had a million dollars, what would they do with it? Are you in touch with them the way you want them to be in touch with you? See, it works both ways. If your whole family has been rushing around, taking each other for granted, then it's time to get to know each other again. And that means talking.

EVERYBODY'S WRONG SOMETIMES

Have you ever been wrong? Don't just skip over this question—even if it is a scary concept. Stop and think about it. When have you been unreasonable— and why? If you can't think of an example, ask a sister, brother or your parents for one. Don't get offended if they *can* remember times that you've been wrong; everyone's wrong sometimes.

So, think about when you've been wrong. How did you feel? What did you say? Was it hard to admit you were wrong? Did you admit it—or did you get angry? Well, if you can be unreasonable, so can other people—including parents! Just because they're adults doesn't mean that they're always reasonable. Maybe they had a bad day or what you're talking about reminds them of something that upsets them or they misunderstand or are just blind on this particular subject. So what? They're human. They can be wrong—and they can change, just like you. Keep talking and you may find some room for agreement.

Another important thing to think about is what to do if you are wrong. Maybe you were unreasonable, and maybe you said things you shouldn't have. What do you do now? Right—apologize! This can be difficult—because *nobody*, but nobody, likes to admit that they're wrong—but it's really important. In addition, an apology makes you look good. It makes you seem confident and mature and can go a long way in convincing your parents that you are growing up. A simple "I'm sorry" should do, although on occasion a card or a small present might make the message come through clearer.

DIFFERENCES DO EXIST

Molly had two friends, Sarah and Kim, who were going camping in a state park by themselves. Sarah's parents were going to drop the girls off Saturday and pick them up Sunday morning. Sarah and Kim really wanted Molly to go with them, but Molly's parents had a different idea.

"I thought they were really unreasonable," said Molly. "They would hardly listen to me at all. They just said no, no, no. I kept trying to explain that we would call in at night, and that it was all okay, but they still said no. So, I said, 'Didn't you ever want to do something like this when you were my age?' And my dad told me about how his parents wouldn't let him ride a bike until he was fourteen, and he thought it was unfair that he couldn't go places on a bike with his friends. So, I asked how come he was doing the same thing to me? And he said it was more important to him that I be safe than that I be happy with him about this decision. I realized then that he wasn't being mean; he wasn't letting me go because he loves me and cares about my safety. I still don't agree, but I feel like he understands me and I understand him better, too."

Your growing up is hard for your parents. They remember when you were a tiny baby, when you really were helpless and needed their protection. They have to learn to adjust to the fact that you are growing up, and that they can let go a little. It wasn't that many years ago when they actually had to *feed* you—you know, with a spoon!—so don't be surprised when they still try to help you with your life. It's because they care!

PEOPLE LIKE DIFFERENT THINGS

Most people think other people will like what they like—it's called projecting. Lisa's mom bought her an expensive scarf as a special present for her birthday. "I really hurt my mom's feelings," said Lisa. "She thought it was a beautiful scarf, but I thought it was just gross. I didn't understand how she could pick out something so ugly."

Jamie's dad kept taking her hunting. "My dad loves hunting, but I hate it," said Jamie. "He thinks it ought to be a big treat for me to go with him, but it's really more like torture. It's not that I don't like being with him; I just don't like killing things. Why doesn't he realize that?"

When people don't understand you, they're not trying to *hurt* you—more likely they think that if they like something, if something is important to them, it will make you happy, too. If you understand this point, it could help you avoid hurting people's feelings. You'll need to find tactful ways to let them know when you're not pleased, and hope that they get the idea after a while.

Sometimes, even after you've discussed things, your parents still will not see eye-to-eye with you. They're entitled to their opinion, just as you're entitled to yours. But both you and your parents should remember one thing—the other person could be right!

GIVE A LITTLE, TAKE A LITTLE

We'll get into the details of what to do when your parents and you just don't agree in the next chapter, but first we'd just like to mention the ideas of compromise and negotiation. You may have noticed that when you disagree with someone, if you both just stand there saying the same things over and over again—surprise, surprise—nothing gets solved. What you need to do is *compromise*, and this is accomplished by *negotiation*.

Suppose you want to be allowed to stay up until 10:00 P.M. and your parents say that 9:00 P.M. is the absolute limit. What do you do? Well, you could go to bed at 9:00 P.M. and then read under your covers until 10:00 P.M., but that won't really solve anything. Try negotiating; suggest 9:30 P.M. as a compromise, and then, once you've shown that you still have enough energy to get through the day, maybe they'll agree to 10:00 P.M. But in any case, you're better off than you were before, *and* you've shown that you can deal with a problem in a mature and rational way.

Michelle has a similar problem:

Dear Smart Talk,

My mom is so old-fashioned, she really drives me crazy. All my friends go to the mall to hang out, but she won't let me go unless she takes me shopping or to a movie. Why can't she see that I'm not a little kid anymore and let me have some fun?

Michelle

Dear Michelle,

Have you looked at it from her point of view? It might help you understand why she feels the way she does. If you want to have more freedom, you need to explain how you feel to your mom, and show her that you can handle the responsibility. Maybe you can come to an agreement where you'll go with your friends for a few hours once a week, and she'll pick you up so she can see for herself what you and your friends are doing. But don't expect her to suddenly treat you like a grown-up. Give her—and yourself—time to let go of old rules.

BEYOND UNDERSTANDING

Kids and parents always have had and always will have different points of view on a lot of things. That doesn't mean you can't talk to each other and love each other and get along. Sometimes, in the rush of growing up, we forget something very important: Conflicts may be very real, but so is the love between parents and children. So when things get tough, here is a list of things to tell your parents (and to remind yourself):

- ✪ *You love them.*

- ✪ *They love you.*

- ✪ *You want to understand them.*

- ✪ *You want them to understand you.*

- ✪ *You want to do the right thing.*

- ✪ *You will listen to them.*

- ✪ *You hope they'll listen to you.*

- ✪ *You know you won't always agree, but you want to be able to talk things out.*

Even if they know these things deep down, hearing them always helps. And it's nice to remind yourself of them every now and then as well.

Let's Make a DEAL

*D*o words ever get in the way when you're talking? If so, you might need a kind of "road map" to help you direct your discussions. That's where the DEAL system comes in. DEAL is actually an acronym (a word made up of the first letters of the words it stands for) which stands for **D**efine, **E**xplain, **A**sk and **L**isten. (We'll explain that more fully below.) The DEAL system is a handy way to make sure you're getting your ideas across. With a little practice, the DEAL system will help you communicate better. It may even help you smooth out those talks with your parents. If you look back on talks where you felt good about how things went, you'll probably find that you used some elements of the DEAL system—and you didn't even know it!

Using the DEAL system doesn't mean you'll always get your parents to agree with your point of view, but it will keep your talks on track. Of course, once you get the hang of it, you won't use it just to talk to your parents—it's great for getting results with friends, teachers and other family members, too! Take the quiz below and see how much you already know about DEALing!

☆☆ COMMUNICATIONS QUIZ ☆☆

1. *It's possible to use too many details when you're talking.*

   True or False.

2. *If you aren't specific about what you mean, you could be misunderstood.*

   True or False.

3. *Just talking isn't communicating—there has to be listening, too.*

   True or False.

4. *It's a good idea to keep the conversation on the topic you started with.*

   True or False.

5. *Listening can be difficult.*

   True or False.

6. *What we seem to be talking about isn't always what we're really talking about.*

   True or False.

7. *Giving feedback is an important part of talking.*

   True or False.

8. *Thinking of what you're going to say next while someone else is talking is not a good idea.*

   True or False.

Scoring:

   They're all true! For a more complete explanation, read on.

30

DEFINE

No, you don't need to use a dictionary to look up words, but you *do* need to understand exactly what it is you want to say. Maybe you think that's pretty obvious—but how often do you tell your mom or dad something, only to have them give you a reply that seems to come from Mars? "But that's not what I mean," you probably say. Well, what *do* you mean? If you don't know, no one else will, either.

Defining isn't always easy. For example, Natalie had spent some time thinking about picking out a new dress for an upcoming party. She thought about trying on lots of dresses and comparing prices, and she pictured herself going shopping with her mother and the two of them buying the dress together.

Natalie was excited about going shopping with her mother and having lunch with her like they were buddies, instead of just mother and daughter. "So, I went into the living room and told her I'd like her to help me buy a dress for the party," Natalie said. "She said great. And then the next evening when she got home from work, she brought me a dress she'd bought on her lunch hour. She was all excited about it, but I was so disappointed I threw it on the floor and said I hated it. We both ended up crying."

No wonder Natalie and her mom were upset—Natalie didn't just want a dress, she wanted to go

Always **define** *what you mean or you could end up confusing everyone—including yourself.*

shopping with her mother. She wanted them to pick out a dress *together*. But she didn't stop to *define*. And Natalie's mother probably forgot that pre-teens and teenagers want to participate in decisions about important things like clothes.

EXPLAIN

Once you've figured out what you want to talk about—*defined*—you have to say it in a way that will get results. Easy, huh? Well, it can be, but there's no guarantee that your parents will understand you if you don't first stop and think about how your words sound to them.

Lynn had received an A on a math test for the first time. She was pleased by how much she had improved in math and wanted to tell her dad all about it, but things didn't turn out the way she expected.

"I started telling my dad how I had a hard time with math, not like my friend Beth, who never even studies," Lynn said. "I told him our teacher always has Beth do examples on the board. But I never get things right on the board, so she never calls on me anymore. Then Dad started criticizing me for always comparing myself to Beth, and he said that if I just worked harder I could do better and that maybe I shouldn't spend so much time on the phone with my friends. Then we both got really mad."

Poor Lynn—and poor Dad! They never even got around to Lynn's A on the test! Lynn didn't stop to think about the best way to *explain* her story.

An important part of explaining is putting your ideas in the right order—just like an essay for English class. Start with the important information and try not to get bogged down with too many small details. Stick to the point: If you put in a lot of extra stuff that doesn't matter, your parents may get overwhelmed just trying to sort things out.

This works both ways: Don't let them get sidetracked, either. If your parents interrupt you and start drifting off the point, you'll have to hang tough. Try saying something like "I'll be glad to talk about that in a minute, but first I'd like to finish explaining this." It won't be easy, especially in the beginning; after all, you've probably spent your whole life doing it the old way. Just give them time and they'll adapt.

ASK

What are you asking for? What do you want your parents to *do* about what you're saying? Are you simply sharing how you feel about something, or do you want their advice? Do you want your parents to do something in particular or just listen sympathetically? Be sure you *say* what you want. Start out by saying "I'd like your help with this," or "I could really use your advice" or "Mom, is it okay if I go to the movies on Tuesday night?" Don't expect your parents to read your mind!

LISTEN

Last but not least, give your parents equal time. After you've finished talking, *listen* to what they have to say. If you don't understand something, you can ask questions to help clarify, but don't interrupt and don't argue—at least, not now. You've had your say: now it's their turn.

Scientists have found that listening is one of the hardest things for people to do. Most of us think of listening as a *passive* activity, like when the radio or television is on but you're actually doing other stuff. But the kind of listening you need to do—the kind the scientists are talking about—takes a lot of concentration and energy. It's called *active listening*, and to do it you have to focus all your attention on what the person you're talking to is saying. An active listener looks the other person in the eye most of the time—and she isn't busy thinking of what she's going to say next. It's hard work, but it pays off. You'll find that when you *actively* listen, the person you're talking to will listen better, too. And that means great communicating!

If you listen closely, you may discover that when your parents raise objections to some of your ideas, you have answers for them! You'll be able to give them information that will help them see your point of view better. You may discover that they've misunderstood something—in spite of all your careful defining and explaining!

And if you've asked for advice, this is the time to really pay attention. It's pretty rude, after all, to ask someone's opinion and then start watching television. Your parents will appreciate your attention, and they'll be more ready to give you advice when you ask some other time.

DEAL Recap

- **Define** exactly what you want to say.
- **Explain** yourself clearly and accurately, without getting sidetracked.
- **Ask** for what you want; don't expect your parents to read your mind.
- **Listen** to their answer.

CHARTING YOUR DEALS

So, that's the DEAL system. Obviously, it'll be easier to use in some cases than in others. Asking permission to go out with your friends to a movie might be easy; telling your parents you're failing a class is going to be hard. The best way to help get the most from DEALing is to use a simple exercise—the DEAL chart.

The following charts will show you how Lisa and her friend Megan used their DEAL charts, just to get you started. Lisa wanted permission to take Spanish lessons after school instead of looking after her little sister, Lauren; Megan wanted to have a big party for her birthday. Here's how they handled it:

Lisa's DEAL chart

What Am I Talking About?	Key Phrases for Explaining.	What Am I Asking For?	What Did They Say?
I want Spanish lessons	Important for school in the future; only top students eligible; no cost	Permission; Lauren to go to play group twice a week	Yes, as long as other studies don't suffer

Megan's DEAL chart

What Am I Talking About?	Key Phrases for Explaining.	What Am I Asking for?	What Did They Say?

First Discussion

A big birthday party	All my friends have invited me to theirs; never had a big party	Permission; Mom to help; swim and cookout at home	No, too expensive; Mom too busy

Second Discussion

Birthday party	Want to pay back friends; celebrate; keep costs and fuss down	Permission; take close friends to skate and eat pizza	Yes!

By now, you probably realize the amazing part about the DEAL system: It's never really over, it just keeps circling around! To use a DEAL chart for your own discussion topics, simply use your journal, draw up your own chart and have fun! After you've listened to what your parents say, you might want to go right back to the beginning and *define* again—maybe changing how you see the situation after hearing your parents' point of view. If you've learned something during the conversation, then you'll be able to use that new insight in your next explanation step. Or maybe you'll see that you can ask for something else and still be satisfied (compromise, remember?). Sometimes you'll do this over and over in one conversation—other times, you may want to take some time to think the subject over and start a new talk later.

But what if you've *defined*, *explained*, *asked* and *listened* a couple of times—and it's still no go? Well, if you're really back where you started—and that's pretty unusual—then at least you've had a good exchange of ideas with your parents, and you'll have to agree to disagree, for now.

But if you keep in mind that the *real* goal is communicating—not just getting what you want—you'll be a winner every time!

DEALing DO's

1. DO be clear about what you want to talk about.

2. DO think about how your words will sound to your parents.

3. DO stick to the point.

4. DO ask for what you want.

5. DO listen actively.

6. DO keep trying!

DEALing DON'Ts

1. DON'T talk before you've figured out what you want to say.

2. DON'T start with the details.

3. DON'T include extra information.

4. DON'T get sidetracked.

5. DON'T expect your parents to guess what you want.

6. DON'T interrupt when you are listening, except to clarify.

7. DON'T stop trying!

Tackling the Toughies

Now, let's face facts. Some things are just plain difficult to talk about. You feel silly or embarrassed about them, or you can tell that your mom or dad does. Or you think your parents will be disappointed in you or will jump to conclusions. Will your mom think you're sneaking drinks if you ask questions about liquor? Will your dad get mad if you tell him that something he does bothers you? Will they think you're silly if you tell them you're scared about something?

There are quite a few subjects that set off instant misunderstandings in almost every family. We call these subjects the "toughies," because they seem to be tough for almost everyone to handle.

THE TOP TEN TOUGHIES

1. Dating
2. Drinking and drugs
3. Menstruation and other changes to your body
4. Grades
5. Money
6. Responsibilities at home
7. Parents' problems
8. Fighting with brothers and sisters
9. Family rules and limits
10. Appearance

YOUR OWN TOP TOUGHIES

There are other toughies as well. You'll probably find that in your family there are certain things that are difficult to talk about, for a variety of reasons.

These are your own personal toughies. You should make a list of these in your journal. If you find this difficult, try keeping track of the things you discuss with your parents for a few months. You might notice that when certain topics come up, a fight almost always follows. Those topics are *your* toughies. Once you've figured them out, keep track of them. Note down the date you discussed them and why. This list can help you figure out what to do about your toughies.

Judy's list may be different from yours, but it should give you an idea of what types of toughies different people have to deal with:

Judy's List

Date	Toughie	Why discussed
9/5	Curfew	Half-hour late
9/8	Home-work	Poor mark in math
9/11	Money	Needed advance on allowance for party at Jill's
9/13	Curfew	Half-hour late
9/13	Family limits	R-rated movie Mom wouldn't let me see
9/14	Curfew	Half-hour late

After seeing how often it came up as a topic, Judy decided to ask for a later curfew. Her parents agreed—if she improved her math marks!

TAMING THE TOUGHIES

The toughies are called toughies because they may *never* be easy to discuss, no matter how good you get at communicating. Of course, some people will have problems with some topics and not with others, and some people might be good at talking about *anything*. But, in general, these topics are *tough*, plain and simple.

If you use the DEAL system, we bet you'll get a better handle on the toughies than you ever thought you could. In fact, talking about the toughies is a particular specialty of the DEAL system, because it helps you keep your discussion on the subject at hand, without dragging in a lot of other stuff that just complicates the discussion and gets people upset. If you think about the times you've talked about the toughies before, you may discover that often the conversation just drifted away from the point, into an argument or another topic—because the toughie was just too tough! DEALing gives you the skills to help keep that from happening.

Take Pam, for example. She was worried because she hadn't gotten her period yet. All her friends had started, and she thought maybe something was

Only talk can tame the toughies, so explain your feelings to those you love.

wrong with her. Her mother had given her some books to read a few years earlier, but Pam and her mom had never really *talked* about the subject, and Pam felt funny bringing it up.

"So, I used the DEAL chart," Pam said. "I said I was worried because I hadn't gotten my period yet, and I asked her if she thought I should see a doctor. She was embarrassed, but she explained that I shouldn't worry, it wasn't that unusual. But she agreed to make me an appointment. I don't think we'll ever have long talks on the subject, but at least it's out in the open now."

Liz also had a big problem—a friend of hers offered her some drugs, and Liz realized that the friend was selling drugs to other kids at school. She didn't know how to tell her parents about it without getting her friend in trouble or making her parents upset.

"I had to tell them, because they could see I was really miserable, but I tried to do it calmly and stick to the subject," said Liz. "They did get upset. They spent a lot of time quizzing me, asking me if I was sure I had never tried any drugs. Then, they called my friend's parents. My friend got into a counseling program, and I guess it's all going to work out okay. But talking about drugs is hard, because everyone gets upset."

Pam and Liz tackled two of the toughies—and came out winners. You can, too!

TOUGHIE TIPS

✪ If you're finding it really difficult to bring the subject up, try writing your parents a letter. After they've read it, you can meet face to face.

✪ If you're wondering whether or not you should talk to your parents about something, you probably should!

✪ If you think a toughie will just go away if you ignore it, you're wrong. You have to talk it out!

WHAT'S GOING ON HERE?

You may have noticed something else when you've talked about the toughies before—sometimes the discussion gets confused but you don't quite know why. Sometimes you don't even know that what you're talking about is a toughie—until it gets out of hand. Did you ever have a blowup with your parents and come away not really knowing what the problem was? All of a sudden, you were yelling and you really didn't know why.

Sometimes the person you're talking to isn't hearing what you think you're saying. Remember the first basic rule of talking: Communication is a two-way street. Not only do you have to say something clearly, but they have to *hear* it clearly, as well. And sometimes it's not just the words people hear, it's *how* they interpret those words that matters.

For example, you may think you're talking about going over to your friend's house for dinner and a sleep-over—but what your mom (who was planning a special dinner) may be hearing is that you don't need her anymore and you'd rather not spend the time with your family. She feels hurt, and you don't know why. Or maybe you tell your dad about how well the soccer team is doing and how hard you are practicing, and what your dad (who cares a lot about your grades) hears is that you are spending more time on sports than on schoolwork. So he starts asking about your grades instead of enjoying your enthusiasm for soccer. You can't figure out why he's being so demanding.

See? It's not always the words themselves. You've got to figure out how your parents—and other people—are interpreting what you say. Try to judge by their answers, and then answer their *real* concerns. Sounds confusing? Well, sort of. That's when the third basic is important: Put yourself in their shoes.

GOING BEYOND THE WORDS

It helps if you remember some of the things that often upset parents, so here's a brief list:

✪ *They're often worried about your safety.*

✪ *They might feel left out (after all, you're probably spending less time with them than you used to).*

✪ *They want you to do well in school so you do well in life.*

✪ *They worry about you growing up too fast.*

✪ *They worry about not being good parents.*

It won't always be easy, but if you really listen, put yourself in their shoes and practice, you'll get better at understanding the intent behind the words.

If you think you hear a mixed message, you can use *feedback* to test your guess. Feedback is when you say what you think the other person is telling you, but in your own words. Then they can either agree or disagree. For example, Sandy's mother was always telling her to clean up her room. "I really couldn't figure it out," said Sandy. "I mean it's not like *her* room is so neat, or anything. But after a while, it dawned on me that she really didn't care about my room, she was worried about *me*. She just wanted me to learn to be responsible for myself. I asked her if this was the case and she said it was! So we had a long talk about responsibility, and I managed to convince her that I could take care of my things. Now she almost never bugs me about my room!"

Sometimes your parents say something, and it just doesn't make sense. Or you know that they're not saying what they really want to say, but you have *no* clue to what's actually on their minds. How are you supposed to guess what's behind the words? And what if you get it wrong? Well, one way to be sure is to ask. If your mom or dad seems to be getting really upset, stop and ask them why. This could make the other person stop and think about what they're really saying. But it might not always work because people (even parents) don't always know what's on their own minds!

FIGURING IT OUT

"When she found out I tasted some beer at a friend's house," said Martha, "my mom just flew off the handle. All I did was taste it, and I mentioned it to her because I was surprised how bad it tasted—I'd never had any before. And she just blew up. I couldn't get her to listen at all."

Martha stuck with it, because she knew that her mother's reaction meant something else was going on. And finally she just asked, "Mom, why is this so upsetting to you? I don't drink, and you don't need to be so worried about me starting. Why are you getting so upset?"

Martha found out that her mother's father had

been a heavy drinker, and that her family had had a lot of trouble because of it. "She was afraid that it would happen again, so she was always worried about my brothers and me drinking," Martha said. "It wasn't really me at all that was upsetting her, it was remembering her own dad. It was a tough talk, but now I understand her better."

Sue's dad was giving her a hard time about her grades. "He kept on at me because I wasn't working hard enough at my schoolwork, and I was getting pretty miserable," Sue said. "I was real busy with play rehearsals at school, and I didn't have enough time to do everything. I couldn't figure out why he was being so hard on me about my grades."

So instead of arguing, Sue asked her dad why the grades were so important to him. "At first he just tried to go over the same old stuff again, like how I was irresponsible and how my brother's grades were so good, but I kept to the point, and finally he said that he knew that grades mattered from personal experience. He had been held back a grade in junior high, and he had been very embarrassed about it. So, when he saw my grades falling, he was worried that I might have the same kind of bad experience he had, and he didn't want that to happen. He was really trying to help me. But wow! Was he doing it wrong!"

Boyfriends and dating can be toughies, too. "My mom and I were having a good talk about some of my friends, when she started saying strange things about Dave," said Barbara. "He's really nice, but she started running him down. I tried defending him, and we started having a big fight. But it didn't seem to make sense, especially when she said I couldn't spend time with him anymore except at school. So, I asked her why she was upset about my being friends with Dave. And it turned out that she thought we were spending *too much* time together, and she was worried that we were getting too serious. She didn't want to say that, but she kept hinting at it, so I said it as feedback and she agreed! Well, Dave and I are just friends, so I told her she had nothing to worry about. She's still worried, I think, but at least it's out in the open, and we can talk about it."

These girls have it figured out! They've learned to listen to what's really going on—and to give feedback or ask for it when they hear confusing messages. And they've learned to listen to themselves, too, to see if they are talking about what they think they are talking about.

Here's a letter from Chrystal, who has found that sometimes it's hard to know exactly what it is that bothers you:

Dear Smart Talk,

I love my dad, but he has an annoying habit that drives me up the wall. He takes food off my plate at dinner. I don't know why it bothers me so much, but it ruins dinner for me. I hate eating with my family because of it. What's going on? We just had a huge fight over it and we said terrible things to each other.

Chrystal

Dear Chrystal,

You've figured out that you're not fighting about the food, and that's a big step. So what is it? How does it make you feel when your dad eats from your plate? We'll bet that to your dad, it's a way of being close, like you're his little girl again. And we bet that to you, it makes you feel that he wants you to *stay* his little girl, instead of realizing that you're growing up. You want to be your own person, with your own food—and your own friends and ideas—and you want him to respect that, right? Think about it. And then use the DEAL system to talk about what you're *really* talking about.

THE TALK TABLE

Here's a handy way to look at what's behind the talk. You'll want to make your own Talk Table in your journal, but here's one from Paula's notebook to get you started. Use yours to note down things your parents say that you think are really about something else—especially if you're having a problem communicating!

53

Talk Table

What They Said	What's Behind It
Clean your room.	They want me to learn to be responsible.
You're not respectful.	They want to know I love them.
Do your homework.	They want me to get good grades and have better choices for college.
Eat your dinner.	They still think I'm a kid sometimes, and they think they have to take care of me—they love me!

Rules and Responsibilities

*T*here are some rather cruel models of child rearing in nature. For example, when baby birds are ready to fly, their parents throw them out of the nest: They either fly or fall, and they get only one chance. Luckily, most human parents take a

55

more gradual approach to helping their children take wing. Although it's a lot easier this way, preteens and teens sometimes get impatient and feel that they're ready for a lot more than their parents think they are. And sometimes they're right!

If you keep track of the topics you discuss with your parents, you might find that the issues of growing up, freedom and responsibility come up again and again. These are very sensitive topics, and you should be sure of exactly what you want before you bring them up. Maybe you want more freedom: to be able to go where you want, with whom you want and come home later. Maybe you want more responsibility: to be trusted with the care of your own room and stuff, to be allowed to make some decisions on your own or to take on an after-school job. Or maybe you just want them to treat you less like a kid, to give you the faith and respect you feel you've earned.

These are all worthwhile aims, but they are also very complex. You might want to come and go as you please, but would you like it if your parents never told you when *they* were going to be home? And what happens if it's your job to do all the shopping, and suddenly you're swamped with homework? We're not saying that you shouldn't ask for more freedom and responsibility, but *think* about what you want first, and then you can present your thoughts in a way that will make your parents far more open to your suggestions.

WORKING IT OUT

Bonnie and Paula both thought long and hard about what they wanted, and worked out plans with their parents. Bonnie really wanted some more responsibility around the house; she felt like her parents still thought of her as a child and if she had some responsibility they would have more faith in her maturity. So she asked her mom and dad to put her in charge of the entertainment schedule for the family—and they did! Now, she gets to pick the movies they rent or go out to see, and suggests trips and other activities for the family. She has to consider suggestions from her two younger brothers, but she's in charge of the family's recreation for the next few months.

"At first, I only suggested things that I wanted, but now I try to suggest movies the boys will like and trips they can enjoy. I suggested that Mom and Dad have a night on their own once in a while, and that I have a sleep-over with friends every so often," Bonnie said. "It's fun to be in charge, but it's a lot of work, too. Once I got too busy at school and didn't get anything planned, so Mom helped me out."

Paula made a new arrangement with her parents so she wouldn't feel like she had to account for every minute. "My folks are wonderful, but they worry about me too much," Paula said. "I had to call them almost every hour on the hour—even if I was just over at a friend's or at the library!—or they would get upset and then we'd fight and they'd ground me. So, we talked about it and now I just tell them where I'll be and when I'll be back and I call if I'll be more than fifteen minutes late. So far it's working—but I know it's hard for them so I try to be extra-considerate. I don't feel so tied down and I love it!"

FINDING THE BALANCE

Lots of the issues that come up about freedom and responsibility really boil down to *setting limits*—deciding which ones are important and which ones are unnecessary. We think setting limits is like being a good citizen—you have rights *and* responsibilities, and you can't have one without the other!

If you feel you're being shortchanged on the freedom side, maybe you should look at the responsibility side and see if you can find a way to demonstrate to your parents that you're ready for a little more freedom. Once you've shown that you're responsible, they'll be more likely to trust you with the freedom.

Let's look at the most common areas for discussion—helping out at home, schoolwork, money and your actions—and see how you can forestall objections. Basically, you are trying to anticipate your parents' objections to your requests and deal with them beforehand. For example, if you want to ask for the freedom to go to the movies with your friends, and you *know* that your parents are going to say that your grades aren't good enough and that you need the time to study—why not get the grades up *first* and then ask? We bet you'll get much less of an argument.

CHORES

Helping out at home is a major issue in any family, and it's also a good way to prove that you are responsible. In some families, pre-teens and teens are expected to do a lot of the cleaning, shopping and taking care of the younger children, while in others the parents take most of the responsibility for running the home. You and your parents need to work out what you both think is reasonable—and stick with it. Once you've shown that you're responsible and conscientious, your parents will feel much more confident about giving you responsible tasks and freedom.

And remember: There are really very few people out there who actually *like* housework. But it has to be done anyway. It's just a part of life. At some point, you'll have your own home and you'll be responsible for keeping it nice; but, until then, doing your share shows your parents that you are responsible and grown-up enough for additional freedom.

SCHOOLWORK

You have to admit that if your school life is falling apart and you can't get your act together to get the homework done and keep the grades in shape, you're not a great bet for more freedom. However, if you do show that you can handle school, then you can easily argue that you could handle a job, more of a social life, etc.

Getting help with your homework is communication, too.

MONEY MATTERS

Does anybody ever have enough money? (We think it's like closet space—you *always* want more, no matter how much you have.) In some families, there's a set allowance for each kid based on age, and that's supposed to cover all the daily stuff. In others, you just ask for what you need. And in some families, you earn it or you don't get it! Again, there's no best system, but if you feel your allowance is a problem, try talking it over with your parents. They may not know what you need.

But before you talk it over with them, make sure *you* know what you need. List all your daily expenses, and anything else you usually buy or want to buy. Then you'll need to look at it from the whole family's point of view. If there's only so much money available, you may not be able to have all the things you've listed. Or maybe you've listed all the things you *want* to have, but not what's necessary or reasonable. And, of course, every parent has a different idea of what is reasonable. Sure, some teenagers get a brand-new car on their sixteenth birthday, but for most families, that's not a reasonable expense. That's why we don't think there's anything like a "fair" allowance—it all depends on the family's situation.

If you've had trouble handling money in the past—coming home with new tapes you've just bought, then having to borrow money for lunch—

you may need to set some priorities for yourself. Try a budget. Or maybe it's time to earn your own money.

One experiment that can be fun—and informative—is for you to sit in when your parents pay their monthly bills. It's a good way for you to see how your parents make their money decisions—and after you see what it takes to run a whole family, you'll have a new view of your own budget. It's also a good way to learn about cash flow—a skill you'll need for your own money management.

ACTIONS COUNT, TOO!

Your daily actions are probably the most important issues when you are considering asking for more freedom or responsibility. Are you on time? Do you keep your word? Are you where you say you'll be when you're supposed to be there? Saying "Oh, I forgot" does not make people want to trust you more—it makes them want to give you more rules to help you remember!

Being responsible can be as simple as phoning home to say you're running late—instead of letting your parents worry! If you run your life responsibly, you'll find people more willing to let you call your own shots.

THE FREEDOMS CHART

Take a look at your responsibilities and freedoms by adding a Freedoms Chart to your journal. This chart is in two parts: The first is a look at your responsibilities and freedoms *now*, the second helps you plan the *changes* you'd like to make. Amanda was surprised at the results of her chart (below): She found out she had more freedoms than she ever knew! Try it—you may be surprised, too!

FREEDOMS CHART

Responsibilities I Have	Freedoms I Have
Food shop	Choose own clothes
Fold clothes from dryer	Plan own free time
Keep room clean	Privacy on phone and in my room
Take phone messages for Dad	
Wash car once a month	Choose my friends
Walk dog	Choose after-school activities
Practice flute	
Do homework/Get good grades	Choose my books, movies, music, etc
Load dishwasher	

Responsibilities I Want	Freedoms I Want
After-school job	Make my own schedule for getting up and going to bed
Cook dinner once a week	Be able to give up flute

Now that you've really *thought* about these topics, go and *talk* about them. Use the DEAL system and have fun! You may not get exactly what you want, but you're sure to be seen as a responsible, deserving person who can think her way through a situation.

FAMILY RULES

Every family has rules. Some families are more formal than others about how the rules are spelled out—but every family has them. Sometimes it's a matter of who sits where at the table, who washes the dishes or how late the television stays on. And some rules are for safety—not leaving appliances on when you're out of the house or not opening the door to strangers when you're home alone.

Rules can help you know what's expected, and they save time in the long run. You don't have to make a decision each time, you just know the rule and follow it. And if there's not a rule, you probably know what it would be—you just know how things are done in your family. Sue would never hang out after school without calling home, but Laura knows that her mother won't worry as long as she's home in an hour, so she sometimes dawdles or stops by a friend's house. Who's right? Both! Their families just have different rules.

CHANGING THE RULES

The important thing about rights and rules is to know when they need to be changed, and to learn to discuss the changes you want in a helpful way. Your parents have the right to make the rules for your family—but you have the right to have your say about those rules.

Sarah and her sister were supposed to do their share of the house cleaning on Saturdays, before they did anything else. They were always getting into trouble about not getting their work done. The problem was that all their friends got together for brunch on Saturday, and that's when the group made plans for the rest of the weekend. "So, we were rushing around trying to get everything done in time—and it was impossible! We finally sat down, explained the situation to our parents and offered a solution. Now we do our chores on Sunday. What an improvement!"

"In my family there was a rule about no phone calls during meals," said Louise. "But my friends always called while we were eating. Sometimes it was really important, but I had to call them back later. There was also a fifteen-minute limit on calls. I thought the phone rules were really unfair." Louise talked to her parents about the phone rules, and they explained that they felt dinner time was family time and it made them feel unwanted if she was always talking to her friends. They also said that they worried that an emergency phone call (from Louise's brother or sister or from her grandparents) wouldn't be able to get through. However, they did agree to extend the fifteen-minute rule to half an hour, as long as there was at least a fifteen-minute break between calls.

Cindy's family's rules chart will give you a look at the rules in one girl's family. Then, take a look at the rules in your family and make your own chart!

FAMILY RULES CHART

Family Rules Now	Changes I'd Like
No phone calls after nine	
Curfew at eight; bed at ten	Curfew at nine
No friends visit when parents aren't home	

Visit Grandma twice a month

No television before homework
is done

No advance on allowance

Allowance for
clothes, too

R-rated movies with permission
only

Don't interrupt Mom when she's
working

When you look at your list, make sure you remember how many freedoms you *do* have. (Look back at your Freedoms Chart and compare the two.) We bet you have a lot more than you thought: Freedoms like being treated with respect by your family, having your own room, deciding what to wear and when to see your friends, and choosing your own television shows and books. But if there are things you still want, talk it over with your parents—using the DEAL system, of course! Maybe your family would like to have a family conference to discuss the subject together. Some families have conferences on a regular basis, like once a month, to discuss plans and problems together.

Changing rules can be as easy as bringing it up. But nothing can happen if nobody knows that there's anything wrong, so you have to talk, talk, talk.

Whose Life Is It, Anyway?

"They're trying to run my life," wailed Mary. "They try to tell me how to do every little thing. They want to pick my clothes, my friends, what I read, even how I cut my hair! Why can't they trust me with a few decisions of my own?"

Decisions are part of growing up. Some are easy and some are hard, but learning to make them for ourselves is an important skill. And Mary's got a point—we all need to learn to make our own decisions.

Should you tell your friend that her new dress—the one she thinks is incredibly hot—is really ugly? Should you tell your math teacher that the guy in the seat next to you cheated on the test? Should you go out for track or softball or concentrate on your grades this year? Should you buy that blue sweater? Should you take summer classes?

What's your DQ? That's your *Decision Quotient*! Find out with this Decision-Maker's Quiz!

☆☆ DECISION-MAKER'S QUIZ ☆☆

1. *Making decisions is easy.*

    True or False.

2. *When you have to make an important decision, you should just do what feels right at the time.*

    True or False.

3. *Asking for advice about decisions just confuses things.*

    True or False.

69

4. *If something is hard for you to decide, you should probably let someone else decide for you.*

   True or False.

5. *You should talk about your decisions with your parents.*

   True or False.

6. *You should be allowed to make your own decisions about how you do your hair or what clothes you wear.*

   True or False.

7. *When your parents make a decision, you should always agree.*

   True or False.

Scoring:

 1. **False**—Some decisions are easy, but others take some thinking through. If they all seem easy to you, maybe you aren't taking them seriously enough.

 2. **False**—A decision should feel right, but a quick decision may mean you overlook important information or other considerations. Take your time with the important ones.

 3. **False**—Sometimes you need advice, and you should ask for it before you make a decision. Maybe

70

it will be a little confusing, but it's important to get the input you need.

4. **False**—You should make the decisions you are comfortable making, but you shouldn't give up just because something is tough. Stick with it!

5. **True**—If it's a major decision or if you just want their input, you should call on your parents for advice.

6. **True**—But you should consider your parents' point of view. They might have some good ideas!

7. **False**—Wouldn't it be nice to always agree? But most families have topics on which they don't see eye-to-eye. The important thing is that you respect your parents' opinions, just as you want them to respect yours.

☆☆☆

MAKING DECISIONS

How do you make your decisions?

Some people are *impulsive*. They just go ahead and do what seems right at the time. Sometimes they don't think things over enough.

Others talk to their friends, and do pretty much

Making decisions can be difficult, but it's the only way to grow.

what their friends think is right, even if they're not too sure about it themselves. These people have a hard time making up their own minds. They are called *followers*.

Being a pre-teen or teenager means making lots of decisions. Sometimes it's hard to know how much you should let other people advise you in making your decisions. And sometimes parents are reluctant to let their kids make any decisions at all.

"My dad is good about talking things over with me," said Chrystal. "But he never pushes me to do what he says. He wants me to decide things for myself."

Sometimes, it's helpful to have advice from parents and friends who know us well. Jean won a scholarship to a special school for gifted students. It was an exciting honor, but it meant she would have a long bus ride every day and would have to leave all her friends—and give up being editor of the newspaper they had started in school. Should she take the scholarship? Her parents advised her to do it. They pointed out that her new school would have interesting extracurricular activities, too, and that Jean would make new friends. Jean hadn't really considered those things before, and she was glad that her parents had brought them up.

Sandra was flattered that popular Beth wanted her to be her best friend—but Beth didn't want Sandra to spend any time with Tiffany, who'd been Sandra's buddy for years. Who should Sandra choose? Sandra asked her parents for their opinion, but made it clear that it was *her* decision.

Talking these kinds of decisions over with your parents can really help—and they will probably be pleased that you value their input.

WHOSE DECISION IS IT?

Only you can make some decisions—but you may find that your parents have a different viewpoint on which decisions you need help with and which you can make on your own.

Who decides whose decision something is?

"Whenever I ask for advice, it's like they take over," said Jane. "I don't ask for my parents' opinion anymore, because then I'm stuck doing whatever they say. I want advice—but I want to make my own decisions."

"Sometimes I wish my parents would give me more advice," said Cathy. "They always say, 'Whatever you think is best' or something like that. I made the swim team, but it meant that I'd have to go to practice every day and to meets on weekends. I wasn't sure that I wanted to spend that much time on my swimming, especially since it meant I wouldn't be able to help my dad rebuild the car we were working on together. I couldn't get them to say anything about it. I was left on my own. It's like they don't really care."

There's no hard and fast rule about what decisions you should make for yourself, and which ones your parents should help with. Try to make the decisions you're comfortable with yourself—but it's a good idea to check with your parents on the major things.

Some kids get in the habit of taking the easy way out—they let their parents decide everything for them. You should be choosing your clothes, planning your free time, taking care of your own responsibilities around the house—unless there's some very good reason you can't. Decision-making is a skill—the more you practice it, the easier it gets.

WHEN YOU DON'T AGREE

Living with decisions your parents don't agree with can be difficult—for them and for you. For example, you and your parents might not agree on your choice of friends. Marcy had two friends her parents just didn't like.

"Nancy and Jill are kind of noisy and silly, but I like to go skating with them," said Marcy. "My parents don't approve of them because they don't care much about school and I'm an A student. They seem so loud and, well, not really like me. But that's what I like about them—I'm real shy and it's easier for me to make friends when I'm skating with them."

After having some arguments, Marcy and her

parents sat down to talk about the issue seriously. Marcy said that she thought she should be able to choose her own friends. Her parents agreed to that as long as she got her homework done and kept her average up. They still don't care for Nancy and Jill, but they let Marcy decide for herself.

Marcy gained additional understanding of her parents' point of view because of what she saw happening to her friend Jenny. Jenny started going around with an older crowd, who were pretty wild. "Jenny says her parents trust her, and she can choose her own friends," said Marcy. "But I think her parents are wrong. Jenny's too young to be out so late, and her average has really fallen. I think she's headed for trouble, but she can't see it. I'm afraid she'll get into drugs if her parents don't help her. So sometimes I think parents have to be strict about friends, even if kids don't agree."

WHEN THERE'S NO RIGHT OR WRONG . . .

There are some areas where parents and kids frequently misunderstand each other. Stuff like grades, appearance, dating, privacy and music. Because they're family stuff, decisions about them have to be made as a family. Let's look at them one by one.

GRADES

Most families are interested in the grades kids get in school because education is so important to getting what you want out of life. Who decides what's an acceptable grade for someone? Obviously everyone can't make all A's! But if you are doing your best and your parents are still worried about your grades, try talking with them about it. If they know you're really trying, they may not care if the grade is an A or a C. Also, there might be something they can do to help. Try telling them what you find difficult and together you might be able to understand the work. Or they might be able to find someone else to help you.

Sometimes parents tend to take good grades for granted. If you think that's happening, let them know how much effort you're putting into your schoolwork. They can't read your mind!

HAIR AND CLOTHES

Some parents have strong feelings about how their kids should wear their hair and what kind of clothes are acceptable for different occasions. And most teens and pre-teens have very strong views about what they should be wearing. Needless to say, these views sometimes differ quite radically, and these differences can cause problems.

There's no doubt about it—it's *your* hair, and *your* body wearing the clothes, and you have a definite right to make some decisions about the way you want to look. But keep in mind that making other people feel upset isn't good for your overall communication with those people—so it's to your advantage to try to understand why they feel the way they do.

Also, there really are reasons behind your parents' point of view. Society at large has standards about how people should dress. Women who work on Wall Street or in conservative businesses rarely wear pants to work (and certainly not jeans). Men in similar places have to wear suits, or at least nice pants and a jacket, and they are expected to cut their hair short. Some jobs require a uniform, others just expect that you'll know what's appropriate to wear. There are rules for kids, too, even young kids. Until the 1960s girls weren't allowed to wear pants to school, and some schools still have a dress code.

Your parents know all these rules, and perhaps they have to live by them themselves. If they seem to want you to follow them, too, it's because they want the best for their children, and they want you to make a good impression on others. But people have different tastes: You may not agree with your parents on what looks good for a given occasion. And your parents are not likely to know about the latest fads and looks—they may think the newest things just look weird!

Try to explain the situation to your parents. Impress upon them that you dress to fit into your group at school, just as they dress to fit into their group of people at work. And explain that if you look different or out of place you'll feel uncomfortable. Try showing them magazines and explaining that what looks strange to them is accepted in your school. You could go shopping together and point out what's being sold and what other teens are wearing. If you disagree on certain things, discuss specifics—like how tight pants can be, and which casual styles are *TOO* casual for school. If you're lucky, you'll never have to do it again.

Another idea is to find out what your mom and dad looked like in high school. Are there any yearbooks or family pictures around? Sit down together and talk about the way kids used to dress and look and how their parents reacted, and you may find they felt then a lot like the way you feel now. And why not give a little—for a family occasion, for instance, maybe you could wear a dress instead of your favorite jeans. You could work out a compromise, where you agree to follow their rules for dressing for certain family occasions, and in exchange they might give you some leeway in what you wear to school.

Be sure you really talk about the issue—use the DEAL system and really listen. Maybe they can accept your clothes choices, but it's important to them that your hair be out of your face, neatly brushed or held back. Or maybe they have just developed a habit of commenting on your appearance—and it's not that big a deal for them, really. Or maybe something about your appearance makes them worry—they think that people who look a certain way will behave a certain way. Find out! And talk about it!

Dear Smart Talk:

My mom is always criticizing my friends, my hair, my clothes—everything about my life. I'm ready to give up. How can I get her to see that it's my life?

Karen

Dear Karen:

First of all, we bet that if you are ready to give up, so is she!

It sounds like you need a good session with the DEAL system. Sort out what you want to talk about—be sure to follow the DEAL system steps because it sounds like you've let the issues build up a lot, and it's likely that the talk will be hard to handle. Don't forget to look at things from her point of view, and remember the Dreadful Exaggerators and the I Factor. Remember that the goal is communicating, and it may take a while to get on track with each other. And then, get talking!

MAKEUP

Makeup is another appearance issue about which you and your parents might disagree. You may think you're old enough to wear as much as you want, and your folks may think you shouldn't wear any. Again, the answer lies in negotiation and compromise. Talk to your mom about how much makeup she feels is appropriate and why. Tell her what other girls in school are wearing. Why not ask her to show you how to apply makeup? You'll get some tried and true advice, and you'll also show your mom that you're serious about looking good, not just being a slave to fads and advertisements.

DATING

This probably comes close to being a toughie. But, have hope, there are ways of dealing with it. The problem probably is that you feel you're old enough to date, and your parents don't agree. To calm their fears, introduce them to the guy you want to go out with so that they can see he's a nice person. Go out in groups so that they feel that you will be safe.

Show pride in your date—introduce him to your parents!

Suggest they drive you and your date to places and pick you up: That way they will be involved and can see that everything is safe and reasonable. If they refuse to listen or to try any of your suggestions, just keep talking! Remember that the main reason they object to your dating is that they don't think you're old enough, and that is changing rapidly. So stay calm, and show them how grown-up you really are.

PRIVACY

Everyone has a right to their own private stuff, but some families have a hard time following through on that idea! We think you should respect other people's privacy—and that they should respect yours. If you feel you aren't getting the privacy you want, think about why parents might seem to be snooping. It's probably because they care about you, and they are worried that something may be wrong that you haven't told them about. So try the DEAL system to clear the air. It'll help.

Sometimes parents respect your privacy in some ways, but seem to ignore it in others. "My mom would never look at my diary," said Cathy. "But she did something else that I thought was almost as bad—she always listened to my phone conversations. And when my friends were over visiting, she'd listen to us talking. I don't really have any secrets, but it kind of drove me nuts not having any privacy, so I talked to her about it, using the DEAL system.

"I told her that even though I didn't have any secrets from her, I didn't like feeling watched, and asked her for more privacy. But I was really surprised by her answer!" said Cathy. "She said she just liked knowing what I was up to. To her, listening wasn't the same as snooping—she was surprised that it bothered me. She just enjoyed feeling like she was included in my life. I never even guessed that she felt that way! So, we agreed that I'd tell her more about what's going on, and she wouldn't try to find out on her own so much."

MUSIC

Kids and parents have been misunderstanding each other's music since long before the phonograph was invented! You're entitled to your own taste in music—but we recommend two guidelines for your musical conduct. First, be considerate—don't blast everyone with your favorites at all hours of the day or night. People trying to concentrate or relax may not want to hear music at that time. And second, don't close your mind to the music other people like—that's just what you accuse them of doing! Just as with food, try a sample of something different once in a while—you may not like it right away, but it may grow on you!

Is it just your "musical manners" that are at fault?

Try to arrive at a workable compromise for when and how you can enjoy your music.

"I was always getting yelled at by my mom for the music I like," said Alice. "She really couldn't stand it, no matter what time I played it. She just wanted it turned off! So, I finally tried the DEAL system. I asked her to spend an afternoon listening to some of my favorites with me, and then I asked her to play some of her favorites. Well, she didn't like my choices and I didn't like hers, but we had a good time anyway. We both really listened to the music we didn't like, and tried to explain to each other why we liked the music we did. We even tried showing how good some songs were to dance to, and ended up dancing all over the living room! We decided to do it once a month or so, to see if we could find some music that we both like. And I agreed to use headphones more, which made Mom very happy!"

If you're having a lot of disagreements with your parents over music, use the DEAL system. Find out what's really going on—are they worried that the music you like is harmful to you in some way? Discuss the lyrics, how the music makes you feel and why you like it. And then listen to their concerns.

It's All Relatives

*F*amilies are great—people who are there when you need them, who you can talk to, who know you and care about you. But sometimes living together can be difficult. Simple day-to-day things can become taxing, and the people you love the most—your family—can become the ones who irritate you the most.

There are a number of issues that people sharing living quarters must deal with. And being part of a family adds still more. When you live with other people, you have to work out a standard of privacy and decide what gets shared and what doesn't. In a family, you also have to contend with issues that are related to whether you have older or younger siblings, how fair certain rules are and, for a lot of you, the special relationship between fathers and daughters.

These topics will probably come up for discussion at one time or another, so it's a good idea to think about them now. That way, when you want to discuss them later, you'll already know how you feel and what you want to say.

MINE, MINE, ALL MINE

Does being in a family mean nothing is private? Renée has a sister who is always going through her things and wearing her clothes. "I don't think it's right, but my parents say that's what families are for. It's one thing when she borrows a hairbrush or a book, but sometimes she wears my shoes and stretches them because her feet are bigger."

Toni was mortified when her brother found a note she'd received from a friend, and read it aloud to their parents. "It was full of private stuff, about how we felt about some boys at school, and about teachers and all. I sure didn't mean for my mom and dad to know about it. They acted like it was funny, but I didn't think it was funny at all."

Your parents may respect your privacy, but getting your brothers and sisters—especially the younger ones—to go along is not easy. They may not understand how much it matters to you. The best way to show them is by example—respect their privacy and they may get the message. And of course, the DEAL system can help you talk it over with them and your parents.

Renée and Toni needed to think about how to communicate their feelings to their families. Renée used the DEAL chart to plan a talk with her sister and parents about sharing. She had to explain to her sister that borrowing without permission is not sharing and it's not okay. In order for it to be sharing, Renée had to agree to it. But first she had to make sure her parents understood the distinction. Once they did, the three of them explained it to her sister.

Toni let her brother know that she's no different from him—he wouldn't like it if someone went through his private stuff, and she doesn't either. She also told her parents how it made her feel when they listened to the note and laughed. They just didn't know how much it mattered to her—until she told them!

WHAT'S YOUR NUMBER?

Sometimes people take on special roles, just because of where they fall in the family order. For example, oldest children often get more responsibility earlier than the younger children, and some parents expect oldest children to be "little adults" and help with the care of the younger ones. This can have advantages—they'll probably trust you more and give you more responsibility—but it can also be a burden. Your brothers or sisters may expect you to always be available to help them with problems or to take them places, and your parents will probably expect you to baby-sit. If you're the oldest, you may occasionally need to remind your parents that you're still a kid!

The youngest child can have the opposite problem—some parents don't want their "baby" to grow up. There are benefits to being the youngest—usually the older kids have blazed the trail, and your parents may not be as strict with you as they were with the older ones. And you have the benefits of older brothers' or sisters' advice—they've been through most of the things you're dealing with now, and they know how it feels! But if you're the youngest, make sure your parents know that you're not really a baby—even the littlest kid gets big!

The real point here is that each of us is an individual. We may be assigned roles because of

Believe it or not, sisters (and brothers) can be your closest friends.

things that have nothing to do with who we really are—like our place in the family—but we need to recognize when those roles are getting in the way of our development and our communication with our parents, and be ready to talk about it.

FAIRNESS

Who decides what's fair? It's not always so easy for families to be fair—sometimes there's just not enough of something to go around, for instance. But sometimes, well, things just *aren't* fair. And then what happens?

"My parents always let my little sister get away with murder," said Pat. "I kill myself to get good grades and she gets C's and they say 'Oh, that's fine, dear.' She's always asking for money and buying clothes and stuff and she never does her chores around the house. They act like anything she does is wonderful, but they're all over me if I try it."

Pat's in a situation that she feels is unfair. She'd like to change the way things are—and that may not be possible. What *is* possible is to change the way she handles the situation. She can let her parents know how she feels. Talking may not change everything—but the important thing is that Pat must communicate with her parents about her feelings. That means talking and more talking!

The DEAL system can really help you talk to your family in situations like these. When Pat fills in her DEAL chart, she'll find that what she's asking for is not that her parents put pressure on her sister to make better grades, but that they show more appreciation for Pat.

If you have a problem with fairness in your family, talk about it! You may find out that other members of the family are willing to see it your way, though they may have a different view. Fairness may be in the eye of the beholder! But you'll never know until you talk it over.

☆☆ FAIR'S FAIR QUIZ ☆☆

1. *You just discovered your older sister has worn your new jeans, and they are ruined because she got them all dirty and tore them. You:*

   a. Call her a jerk and tell her you hate her.

   b. Refuse to talk to her, then get something of hers and ruin it.

   c. Go to your mom and tell her about what your sister did.

   d. Explain to your sister how you feel, and let her know that if she can't respect your privacy the two of you will have to talk to your parents about some new rules.

2. *Your parents buy a bike for your brother, after they've told you they can't buy you a CD player. You:*

   a. Tell your parents they are mean and unfair.

   b. Decide to pay them back by failing your math test.

   c. Tell your brother you hate him.

   d. Explain to your parents that you feel hurt because it seems like they favor your brother.

3. *Your sister, who's two years older, gets twice as much allowance as you do. You think you should get the same, but your parents say no. You:*

   a. Tell your parents they always favor your sister.

   b. Keep the change when you go to the store for your mom.

   c. Tell your sister she's a jerk.

   d. Explain to your parents what you need the money for, show them your weekly budget and discuss why you feel you should get more money.

4. *Your brother is watching a movie on television and you want to watch the big tennis match that you've waited all week for. You:*

   a. Tell your brother he's a hog.

   b. Switch the channel and start a fight.

   c. Tell your parents your brother is a hog and he never lets you watch anything on television.

   d. Explain to your brother that you want to watch the tennis match, and try to work out a compromise.

5. *Your brother makes fun of your new haircut. You:*

   a. Tell him he always looks like a jerk anyway.

   b. Throw a magazine at him.

   c. Tell your parents that your brother is teasing you.

   d. Tell him that it makes you feel bad when he teases you, and you'd like him to stop.

☆☆☆

Scoring:

If you answered mostly a's: You're saying words, but not communicating. Try the DEAL system, and practice saying what you want to say.

If you answered mostly b's: You've mastered the nonverbal approach—too bad it's a loser. Give it up and start talking.

If you answered mostly c's: You're talking to the wrong people—communicate with the people who can help make a change!

If you answered mostly d's: You've got it! And we bet you find things are going better than before!

☆☆☆

DADS AND DAUGHTERS

Girls often find it easier to talk to their mothers than to their fathers. But if Mom's not around, it's Dad's turn. There may be some things you just don't feel comfortable discussing with your father— clothes, perhaps, or the changes that are happening to your body or maybe just how you feel about boys and dating. But it's important to keep those communication lines open between you and your father.

Try discussing with him the things that bother you. Start with the small stuff and work your way up to the toughies. You'll find that he has a lot to say and a lot of good advice to give. If he seems uncomfortable at first, just keep trying. He'll get the hang of it eventually!

It's worth the effort. Having your father as your friend is a wonderful thing, and can make your teen years much easier.

Talking Through the
Hard Times

*A*ll families go through hard times. Parents divorce, and divorced parents remarry. A family member becomes seriously ill or gets injured or dies. Sometimes things get so bad, it's difficult to believe they're ever going to get better.

If your family is going through one of these changes, you might not feel great for a while. You might feel very unlike yourself: Everything and everybody may look a little different; things that were fun may not be as fun anymore. You may not feel like trusting anyone because you are feeling angry, sad or hurt.

And, just when you want to go off into a corner and be alone with your misery, what do we want you to do? That's right—we want you to keep talking! Talking will help you, and it will help your family, too. You're not going through this change alone. There are other people in this with you, and even if it's terribly hard, you all have to keep in touch with each other's feelings. And that means talking, even when it hurts.

IT'S ALL RIGHT TO CRY

You may find that some of your talking turns into crying—that's okay. Crying is communicating. It lets other people know you're hurting or feeling scared. And you shouldn't be surprised to see others in your family cry—even the grown-ups. Crying is normal: It's an important way for people to deal with their strongest feelings. People cry until they don't need to cry anymore, and then they begin to feel better. If you try to skip the crying phase by holding it back,

Crying is communicating, so never be afraid to let some-one see your tears.

it will take you longer to work through the pain, anger and grief you may feel. So go ahead and let it all out.

During the bad times you might find that sometimes every discussion turns into a yelling contest. This is not helpful, and you have to try to find a way to stop it. If you find yourself starting to yell, stop and ask yourself why. Are you uncomfortable? Have you just run into a toughie? Take a few deep breaths and calm down. Force yourself to speak calmly and to think about what you're saying.

If your parents start yelling, it is even more important that you don't. Stay calm, speak softly. This should help quiet things down. If that doesn't work, try pointing out to them (in a non-accusatory way) that they are yelling and it would be more constructive to discuss things in a quieter fashion. You might also suggest that you are all too upset to discuss the topic at the moment and that maybe you should try talking about it later. By the time you resume your discussion, everyone should be much calmer.

LEARNING TO GO ON

Some changes are absolute, and you may never understand why or how they happened. It's not easy to understand or accept death or other permanent changes. But part of growing up is learning to go on, even when you don't particularly feel like it. Give yourself time to come to terms with change and grief. And when you've dealt with it, and recovered from the pain and sorrow, don't be afraid to go on and don't feel guilty. Being miserable won't help anyone or make things go back to the way they were. You have to live your life the best way you can in the circumstances you have. Don't let sadness become a habit. Use it as a tool, and then move on. And remember, when you are sad, find somebody to talk to.

DIVORCE

"When my parents told me they were getting a divorce, I just went into shock," said Leslie. "I knew they'd been fighting a lot, but I couldn't believe this was happening to me. My little sister, Joanne, didn't really understand, but I felt like my life was over. I didn't know where I would live or if they would still love me. I was really hurt and angry."

Leslie's parents took their daughters to a counselor, and all four of them talked about what was happening. They continued to see the counselor together for a few months, and then Leslie went to sessions on her own. "The counseling helped a lot," said Leslie. "It helped us all talk to each other about what was happening, and then later it gave me someone to talk to who wouldn't take sides. My parents were so upset that they couldn't really focus on me—but the counselor was calm and was there just for *me*. It was still awful, and I miss my dad now that I live with my mother, but I don't feel so alone. I've been able to help Joanne a lot, and be a better sister to her. I guess I'll be okay, after all!"

Alison wasn't as lucky—her parents were so angry and upset that the divorce was very difficult for everyone. "They fought and yelled and called each other names all the time," Alison remembers. "They wanted my brothers and me to choose sides. It was awful going home. But my brothers and I decided we just wouldn't get involved in their problem. We kids talked a lot, and just tried to really be good to each other and help each other.

"My grades dropped a little, and I was sick a lot, but mainly I got through it okay. We stay with my dad, and my mom lives pretty close, so we didn't have to change schools or anything. If I hadn't had my brothers, though, I wouldn't have done very well. I guess I would have had to go to my friends because you just can't go through something this hard alone. You have to talk to someone."

Particularly in the case of divorce, your parents might be too upset to really listen to you. It might be a good idea to find some other adult to talk to, or other people in your family like siblings or cousins. And don't worry about your parents too much—they'll be all right in the end.

STEPFAMILIES

"My dad's new wife is okay, but she's not my mom. She doesn't seem to have anything to do with me, really. She's just there. I don't hate her, but I wish I didn't have to live with her," said Penny.

"My stepsister Alice is a whiz—she gets great grades and is really popular. I feel like a failure compared to her," said Joyce.

"My stepfather is great, but he seems very distant. It's like he thinks since he's not my *real* dad he shouldn't tell me what he thinks or how he feels. I wish he'd open up more so I could be closer to him," said Tricia.

Getting in step with a stepfamily can be a big challenge. Suddenly, your dad has a wife who's not your mom, or your mom has a husband who's not your dad. You're not too sure where you fit into the picture. And if there are other kids involved—then, whoosh! Instant brothers and sisters! Why do you have to deal with all these strangers? You never asked for any of it!

All families have their tensions—their pluses and minuses—and stepfamilies are no exception. Sometimes it feels a bit trickier for us to talk to each other honestly in a stepfamily because it seems easier for people we don't know very well to misunderstand our intentions. There can be a sort of "Well, we're not *really* related, anyway" feeling underlying everything that makes people hesitate to open up. But talking is especially important in a stepfamily, and the DEAL system can really help. Start off slowly, especially if you haven't been talking a lot before, but *do* get started.

Penny would be doing herself and her stepmother a favor if she used the DEAL system to discuss her feelings. She needs to let both her dad and her stepmother know how she feels. If she wants a closer relationship with her stepmother, she'll have to talk about it. The DEAL system would also help her figure out if there's something she wants her dad or stepmother to do, and help her ask them for it.

"I finally felt so bad about my stepsister, I talked to my dad about it," said Joyce. "He really helped by telling me a lot of good things about myself, and then he told me that Alice isn't perfect. But he said that anyone can make themselves feel bad by comparing themselves to someone else. I guess the main thing is he told me he loved me—and that's what I really needed to hear!"

Tricia tried the DEAL system to get closer to her stepfather. "I used the DEAL chart to get ready because I didn't want to say anything that might turn him off," said Tricia. "I wanted to talk about being closer to him, and I thought my key words were that I loved him and that I was glad he was my stepfather. I asked him if we could spend more time together. I was worried that he might think I was criticizing him. But he was really happy about what I said. We decided to talk about books for a while after dinner, instead of watching television. It's still a little awkward, but it's a start!"

Tricia did a great job using the DEAL system to help her get closer to her stepfather. She also found out that communicating doesn't happen all at once—once you get started, you have to *keep talking*.

THE SINGLE-PARENT HOME

Lots of kids have one parent, or split their time between two separate homes with one parent in each. Some things work differently in a single-parent family. There will be a lot more stress on your parent, and there may be less time for family activities if one person is working full-time and also trying to care for the family. Single parents need help and support—and that's where you come in! You can pitch in and help out; you probably already do. It's important to sit down together from time to time and go over the list of chores and other matters and make sure you're all satisfied with how things are going, and to keep in touch with each other's feelings.

But as much as you need to help out, you still need time and space for yourself. Sometimes, kids in a single-parent family try to do too much and feel they have to be perfect. Well, nobody's perfect. And it doesn't matter! Be sure you find time to really talk with your parent—that's what matters most.

WHEN YOUR PARENTS ARE IN TROUBLE

Sometimes parents have problems that are so serious they become problems for the whole family. If a parent loses a job or becomes emotionally or physically ill, it may have a major impact on the whole family—including you. And if your parents are having problems in their marriage, you are bound to be involved. How can you handle a parent's problems?

The answer is, you can't. Your parents' problems are *their* problems. You can only deal with your own problems, and you may need help to do that. After all, you are not a grown-up—you're still learning! If your parents are caught up in their own problems, they may not see that you have problems of your own. In this case, you might seek help outside the family.

WHEN YOU NEED EXTRA HELP

In some situations you need to get help, and *fast*. If your parents are abusing drugs or alcohol, if they are hitting each other or you or your brothers or sisters, if anyone is touching you in ways you don't like or if you feel depressed all the time, then you *must*, absolutely *must*, find an adult who can help you. A teacher or counselor is a good choice, and if the first person you talk to won't listen or doesn't understand, try someone else. As a last resort, you can call the police and ask them what to do. But you must not live in fear. You must get help for yourself. You are not the only one in this situation, and *it is not your fault*. If you're strong and determined, you'll make it through even this—as long as you keep talking.

GET EXTRA HELP IF:

- ✪ A parent is drinking
- ✪ A parent is abusing drugs
- ✪ People are hitting each other
- ✪ Anyone is touching you in ways you don't like
- ✪ You feel sad all the time

YOU'VE TRIED EVERYTHING

Does the phrase "blue in the face" ring a bell? As in, you've tried talking until you're b.i.t.f. and they *still* don't understand? They still don't listen? Well, the sad truth is that some parents are just poor communicators. And some just won't get much better, no matter what you do. If you've been using the DEAL system, we bet that your relationship with your parents is *better* than it used to be, but if it

107

was really poor to start with, that may not be enough of an improvement.

You can get very frustrated trying to talk to someone who isn't really listening to you. So what can you do? You probably know the answer by now—keep talking!

FIND A HELPER

But that's not all: You have to keep talking to your parents, but you also have to accept the fact that they have their limitations. Be realistic. Try not to get upset with your parents for being the way they are—they aren't doing it on purpose, and they probably are trying their best. You just need something—and someone—different. You may have to take charge of your own life, and find an adult or two who will be there for you when you need them.

Finding an adult you can trust and talk to is very important, and it may not be easy. If you don't have a family member who can help—an older brother, sister or cousin, or an uncle or aunt—you might look to neighbors, teachers, friends' parents, counselors or religious leaders. If it's someone you see a lot, you may be able to just spend time with the person, and a relationship will develop naturally. But if it's someone you don't normally see on a regular basis, you may need to explain what you need.

Once you've found an adult who's easy to talk to, you might even want to set up a regular meeting time, or plan activities you can share. It doesn't have to be long or uncomfortable—maybe just a walk in the park, doing the laundry at the laundromat, playing duets, anything!

Top Talker Tips

*D*oes good communicating make a difference? You bet it does! In this chapter, we're going to explore the way some "top talkers" made it work for them!

LISTENING AND LEARNING

What's the hardest part of learning to be a top talker? Most top talkers agree that *listening* was the biggest challenge. "The first thing I had to learn was how to listen," said Marti. "Before I used the DEAL system, I never really listened at all. I *thought* I was listening, but really I had my mind made up that things should be my way, and I was just waiting for my turn. And that's not listening."

"I had to learn to listen, too," said Jenny. "But the biggest problem I had was learning to say what I meant. I used to use a lot of words, but I didn't spend much time choosing them. I just ran on and on, and sometimes I probably didn't make a lot of sense. It wasn't very good communicating—but I didn't know it!"

"That's what happened to me," said Tamara. "I thought it was my parents' job to understand *me*—I didn't think I had to spend any time trying to understand *them*. Boy, was I wrong!"

How did they change? "Just understanding what communicating was all about really changed everything," said Marti. "I used my journal so I'd be really focused on what I was doing when I was talking. Until you've tried it, you can't believe how much using the DEAL chart before a discussion can help!"

DEAL YOUR WAY TO STRENGTH

Marti, Jenny and Tamara have each used the DEAL system to tackle some hard problems and tame some toughies in their families. Let's see how they've made it work for them.

"Before I used the DEAL system, I would just say whatever came into my head and if Mom didn't agree, I'd get mad," said Jenny. "We spent a lot of time arguing. But the DEAL system made me really look at what I was saying. I got better at saying what I wanted and asking for it, and listening to Mom's answers. But then, I got into a situation where I was really glad I knew how to talk to her."

Jenny's little brother Tom became very ill, and it was a hard time for the whole family. Everything about the family's life was disrupted, and no one had much time or energy for anything except trying to get Tom better. "I really needed my mom a lot, and she needed me, too. If I hadn't been able to talk with her, everything would have been awful," said Jenny. "A lot of the time she was impatient and cranky with me. But because I knew how to listen for what's behind the words, I knew she wasn't really mad at me, she was scared about Tom. So, I could tell her that I knew she was upset about Tom, and that I understood. It was a hard time, but being able to talk really helped get us through it."

TACKLING A TOUGHIE

Marti had a toughie on her hands—and was she ever glad she knew how to DEAL! "My best friend Liz started dating, and she wanted me to double with her and her boyfriend, Alan," said Marti. "She was spending all her time with him and I felt like she would stop being my friend if I couldn't go out, too. But my parents wouldn't let me.

"They said I was too young to date, and then they wanted me to stop being friends with Liz, because they were afraid she was getting too wild," said Marti. "We just couldn't agree at all. Then I realized I'd made it worse by not talking clearly. I hadn't used feedback to make sure they understood what I meant. When I said the word 'date,' my parents got worried. So I did a DEAL chart, and really focused on my words.

"I told them I wanted to stay friends with Liz, and that I wanted to go out with her and Alan and another boy *in a group*. I told them that we were all just good friends," Marti said. "It sounds easy, but it was a tough discussion, because we'd had so many arguments about the subject. They finally suggested some ways I could get together with Liz, Alan and another boy that they'd approve of—like everyone coming to our house for dinner and a movie, or going skating together or spending an afternoon at the mall. That way Liz could have her date, and I'd still have my friend. It worked!"

TOUGHER STILL

Tamara and her mom were watching a video together when the movie they'd selected turned out to have an explicit love scene.

"I could tell my mom was really uncomfortable, and I was pretty embarrassed, too," said Tamara. "We didn't really want to watch the movie, but I kind of wanted to talk to her about sex because, well, she never says anything about it to me and it was on our minds at the time. I figured I'd probably never have a better chance. So I tried to think about how to DEAL it—and since I'd practiced DEALing on a lot of other things, it wasn't as hard as I thought it would be.

"I asked Mom if we could talk a little," said Tamara. "I told her I didn't really want more information, since I get that at school. I just wanted to know if she had been as nervous as I am about the subject when she was my age, and if it was okay to feel confused about it like I do.

"It was hard to get her talking, but I knew that if I asked questions and stayed on the subject, we'd both feel more comfortable," said Tamara. "We ended up having a pretty good talk. She made me feel like I was okay, and that it was okay to talk with her. I think it'll be easier to talk about important things in the future, since we've kind of broken the ice. Even though it was hard to do, I'm sure glad I tried. There's some stuff you really want to hear from your mom, not someone else!"

DEALING DECISIONS

Marti ran into some problems when she announced she wanted to change schools. "My older sister went to a private school and she loved it, so I went there, too," said Marti. "But after a year, I knew it wasn't for me. First of all, I missed my friends. But mainly the problem was that the school really emphasized math and science, and I'm interested in art and languages. Because I was always struggling to keep up in math, I had to let my art classes go and I couldn't participate in the Spanish club. I didn't enjoy the school at all.

"I knew my parents would be disappointed that I wanted to switch schools, but I also knew they wouldn't be surprised. They'd seen that I was unhappy," said Marti. "What I really wanted them to know was that I wasn't giving up: It just wasn't my kind of place. The public school was a better place for me. So, I used the DEAL chart to get ready. I told them that I wanted to change schools so that I could pursue the things that I cared about. I said that I wanted to work hard at my art and languages and I couldn't do that at the private school.

"They didn't agree. They said the private school was a better school," said Marti. "I told them I didn't think it was better for *me*, because it didn't let me do the things that matter to me. But I tried to understand their feelings, too. They really thought it was important to stay where I was. In the end, we agreed I'd go another year, and take art classes at a gallery on Saturdays. I didn't get what I wanted, but now we understand each other better, and they've agreed that at the end of the year they'll let me make the decision. And at least I'll have the art classes now!"

CHANGING THE RULES

Tamara wanted to change some family rules. "I've had to do the laundry in our family for the past four years. I sort it, wash it, dry it and put it away," said Tamara. "My little sister only has to vacuum once a week, but I have a lot of other jobs, too. And if I want to go to the movies on the weekend, I have to take her with me. I thought the time had come for my sister to have more responsibility and for me to have more freedom to see friends or do my school-work. I wanted to suggest to my parents that my sister and I split the laundry—one of us sort and wash, the other dry and put away. I also thought they should realize that she was old enough to go to the movies with her friends.

"I chose my key words carefully, because I didn't want them to think I was trying to get out of anything or that I didn't like my sister. I said that I thought we should look at how responsibilities were assigned, because we'd had the same jobs for a long time and we had both grown up a lot. I explained that Gwen was old enough to do more—and to go places without me," Tamara said. "They partly agreed with me—now my sister helps with the laundry, and I don't have to take her with me everywhere I go. But now I also have to do some ironing and water all the house plants!"

SHARING YOUR KNOWLEDGE

"My mom had some bad communicating habits," said Jenny. "I'd learned not to use the Dreadful Exaggerators and to remember the I Factor, but she would talk to me about how I *always* did this or *never* did that and that I didn't care what she said and stuff like that.

"I tried to get her to see what she was doing by not doing it myself anymore, but that didn't seem to work," said Jenny. "So, I talked to her about it. I told her that when she used *always* and *never* and talked about what I was doing instead of what she wanted it got in the way of us understanding each other. She got annoyed at first, but I stuck with it. I told her that what I really wanted was for us to be able to talk to each other better, and that was why I brought it up. She finally started listening and she understood.

"And I found out that she feels like my brother and I ignore her and make her tell us everything three or four times before we do it. She feels very frustrated. I realized it was true—I'd gotten in the habit of not paying attention to what she said because of the way she said it. So, I wasn't communicating very well, either! We've improved our communication since we had our talk, and am I glad! My mom is great!"

DOES TALKING MATTER?

Do you really want to spend your time doing all this talking? Are you wondering if it's worth it? Well, the top talkers say it is. "Before I learned to communicate better, my parents and I hardly ever had a good talk," said Tamara. "We just kind of checked in about what was going on; you know, schedules and what's for dinner and stuff like that. But we hardly ever took the time to really talk about how we were feeling about things. And we had a lot of pointless arguments."

"My mom and I were always bickering, too," agreed Jenny. "I mean just silly things, but it made us both feel bad. When I started communicating better, we not only got along better, we had more time to talk—because we weren't wasting our time on subjects that were going nowhere."

"I think one of the best parts of communicating is that you feel like you've got a new friend," said Marti. "It's great when you start to understand your mom or dad, to realize how they see things and why they act the way they do sometimes. I never used to see their point of view on things. Now my dad and I have good talks about what's on *his* mind, too, not just my problems. That's real communicating, when both of us find out new things about the other. It's great!"

Worth it? These three say YES—definitely!

Let communication make you a stronger, happier person!

THE VIEW FROM THE TOP

So, that's how the top talkers do it: There aren't any secrets at all; just learn the basics and practice the skills. And the results—terrific!

Did you notice a pattern? It's pretty obvious—these girls really put communication to work for them! They think about what they're going to say and they listen to the other person. They've mastered DEALing and use it all the time. They don't always get what they want, but they don't let that stop them from talking—even about the toughies!

Is it hard?

Yes!

Can you do it, too?

Absolutely!

DO's for Top Talkers

1. DO learn to really listen.

2. DO think about what you're saying.

3. DO remember you may not get what you want.

4. DO look at things from your parents' point of view.

5. DO respect the opinions of others.

6. DO listen for what's behind the words.

7. DO be willing to go along with your parents' decision.

8. DO pick a good time to talk.

9. DO keep communicating!

DON'Ts for Top Talkers

1. DON'T use the Dreadful Exaggerators or forget the I Factor.

2. DON'T forget to use feedback to be sure you're understanding.

3. DON'T assume you're always right.

4. DON'T be afraid to tackle the toughies.

5. DON'T make communicating a contest.

6. DON'T ignore advice you've asked for.

7. DON'T expect to always agree.

8. DON'T forget they love you!

Last Words

What have we been talking about? Talking!
And when you think about it, most of the famous people you can name are famous because they use words carefully and communicate clearly.

You probably know someone—a teacher or friend,

or, if you're lucky, a family member—who is a good communicator: Someone who always seems to understand you and know how you're feeling, someone who just makes you feel better. People like this can really help us understand ourselves—sometimes they even know what we're feeling before we do! And they're usually good at giving advice, because when you talk to them it almost feels like you're thinking out loud. Family members are particularly good at this because they know you so well.

There's no doubt that all of us like people who are good communicators—they are the people we like to be around, the people who make us feel good. What's the secret of being a good communicator?

It's no secret: It's lots of little things. It starts with a genuine interest in the other person, and it uses a lot of special skills.

But you know this already. You know that communicating is a two-way process, and that the DEAL system can help make communicating easier and better. You know about the basics, the Dreadful Exaggerators and the I Factor, and you know how to listen for the meanings behind the words and use feedback.

It's not easy. Successful communicating takes work and practice and determination. But it's worth the trouble it takes, because it brings us closer to the people we care about and the dreams we pursue. Our families are the best friends we have, the most important people in our lives. It's worth taking the time to learn to talk to them, and to learn to hear all the ways they say they care about us.

Happy communicating!

SMART TALK Has It All!

Some of the best tips for fashion, fun and friendship
are in the Smart Talk series. Learn how to look and
feel your greatest, create your own personal style,
and show the world the great new you! Smart Talk
points the way:

Skin Deep
Looking Good
Eating Pretty
Feeling Fit
Finishing Touches—Manners with Style
Now You're Talking—Winning with Words
Dream Rooms—Decorating with Flair
Great Parties—How to Plan Them
How to Make (and Keep) Friends